Destiny

It is not predefined we make them.

AKSHAT PRIYADARSHI

ISBN 978-93-5458-814-3
© AKSHAT PRIYADARSHI 2021
Published in India 2021 by Pencil

A brand of
One Point Six Technologies Pvt. Ltd.
123, Building J2, Shram Seva Premises,
Wadala Truck Terminal, Wadala (E)
Mumbai 400037, Maharashtra, INDIA
E connect@thepencilapp.com
W www.thepencilapp.com

DISCLAIMER: *This is a work of fiction. Names, characters, places, events and incidents are the products of the author's imagination. The opinions expressed in this book do not seek to reflect the views of the Publisher.*

Author biography

*This book is presented by the author "Akshat Priyadarshi". He is born in the capital city of Jharkhand on 21 July, India. He loves writing and reading fictitious stories, and presenting them before the readers. Furthermore, he has created a fictitious story in front of the readers to glee their minds and to make them understand the real side of their life. In his first book **"Destiny"** he presents a fictitious story in front of the readers describing the harsh life of a family and journey of transformation. All the characters mentioned in the story are created by imagination by the author, Akshat has spent the last decade reading and writing fiction novels giving her characters a palpable spark! His latest work is the sequel to his debut novel, **"Destiny"**.*

CONTENTS

Introduction

This book is created by the imagination. All the characters used in this book are created by the author to pleasure the reader's mind. This book is written by the author in a very simple style so that everyone could understand it clearly and enjoyed the glory and pleasure of a fictitious novel. This book is not for a particular age group, rather readers of all age groups can enjoy the fiction of this novel. In his first book **"Destiny"** *he presents a fictitious story in front of the readers describing the harsh life of a family and the journey of transformation from a small village to a big city.*

During this journey of the family, a lot of hurdles came in their life, but they never look back.

The author also made the reader realize that one can achieve anything in life, if he continuously gives his best in it, and work with full passion and dedication, apart from the struggle the family also faced betrayal from the city people, but they never lose hope. He also made the readers learn a lot from the context of the story by **describing hard work in life, struggle, benefits of good friend zone, all** *in a single story.*

Enjoy the fiction story written by the author **"AKSHAT PRIYADARSHI"**

CHARACTERS OF THE STORY

Bill	*Head of Family*
Jennifer	*Wife of Bill*
Sam	*One of Bill's Collague*
Daisy	*Daughter Of Bill and Jennifer*
Samson	*Daisy's Life partner*
Alex	*Father of Samson*
Oliver	*Son of Daisy*

The Beginning

The story begins with the scene of a small village in the morning, which is very different from that of a city.

Chirping of birds, fresh atmosphere,

the pollution-free environment better describes

the glimpse of village morning. It can make anybody

obsessive to eulogize its

beauty, apart from the beauty,

*the ordinary life of natives is very simple.
They are free from the hustle and bustle*

of city life.

Natives are mostly engaged in agriculture practices, but there was a family whose thought was different from the natives of the village, This was Bill and his family who used to live in the village from his birth itself, and in later too settled there with his wife Jennifer and his daughter Daisy. Bill used to work in his field which he has from his descendant and spend most of the time growing various crops in it. Both Bill and his family were happy from the little money which Bill used to earn for a living, but despite all this, Bill never felt satisfied with his work, as he was a literate person he understands that the city will bring more opportunity in their life then living in a village, as a result, Bill discussed this issue with his wife and daughter.

After discussing the issue with his daughter and better-half,both reacted opposite to each other,

On one side Daisy was very happy to listen that they are going to start their new journey of life in a city, where she will have good friends, good life, good education, and many more.On the other side, Jennifer was contrary in this respect.She reacts negatively to this proposal and said, Life in the city is pretty very good, we have ample opportunity to work, but at the same time living a good life in the city is quite difficult than living in the village. But since Bill was on his word and not was in any condition to listen to his better half. With much late-night conversation and discussion with his better half, he finally succeeded in convincing her.Finally, they started their new journey of life by forgetting all the past experiences which they have before.

SUMMARY OF CHAPTER 1

The story is about Bill, a small farmer who used to live with his wife Jennifer and daughter Daisy in a village. The village and its people were backwords in every respect, as most of the natives were mostly engaged in agriculture practices. But Bill never felt satisfied with his work, as he was a literate person he understands that the city will bring more opportunity in their life than living in a village, as a result, he drops his idea to live rest of his life in the village for their future.

Hardship of Being in a City

*In search of a good city Bill came across a **"Domino City"**, he makes up his mind to stay there rest of his life so that he could bring a drastic change in their life. Domino City not only brings opportunity in the life of Bill's family but rather also helps them to acquire a good way of living, improve their communication skills and get to know various perks of being in a city. Since Bill and his family was new in the city so it was a little difficult for him to find a job for his living, Several months passed, but it was getting difficult for Bill to find a permanent job, day by day it was getting tougher for Bill and his family to live in a city. But soon after many hardships and struggle Bill finally find a permanent job as a Mechanical Engineer in a big factory. This was the turning point for Bill's family because after this the family never face any financial crises. Bill, Jennifer, and their daughter Daisy soon started to make new friends, gradually their standard of living increased, soon they become familiar with the city. One night while working late in the factory, one of his colleagues **"Sam"**tell him about the **"Waterfalls Middle School"**.He further said that "The waterfalls Middle school not only make children handle all the kinds of stuffs from an academic point of you, rather the school help children to develop overall personality". By listening to this Bill make up his mind to admit Daisy in "Waterfalls Middle School".But the fees of "Waterfalls Middle School" made him worried every time, but still, he wanted Daisy to be a part of it. On the entire journey of returning home, he keeps himself busy thinking about Daisy.*

*The Next day, few men from the **"Global Corporation Company"**came to the factory for the inspection about the work. While inspection they came across a man who was so busy in his work draws their attention, he performs the work with firm determination, this was Bill. Officers called Bill at their office for knowing him more. Sam acts as a messsenger for this. Bill was scared that he is going to lose his job, but with a positive attitude, he entered the room. Almost half an hour, officers interrogate Bill about the work. The Officer finds a different kind of spark in him, so they decided to check his honesty. The officers drop a bunch of money near Bill, to find out how he reacts?*

He reacts positively and told the officer with a kind gesture that

"a bunch of money has been mistakenly fallen from your pocket officer".

This kind gesture attitude impressed all the inspection officers on the scene, They realized that this was not the right place for Bill, he deserves much better than this. The Next day he was called to the headquarters of Global Corporation Company for a meeting. He was the first employee from the factory who was called to the headquarter for a meeting. In the meeting, there was an inspection officer along with some seniors officers who interviewed Bill. After much discussion the team members finally offer a job with a good salary at the headquarters, Bill didn't realize that it was all a reality and accepted the proposal of the job since he has to choose Waterfalls Middle School for Daisy.

SUMMARY OF CHAPTER 2

While moving in search of a good city Bill and his family came across Domino city, in the hope to bring a drastic change in their life. Later, they too succeeded in achieving all, but initially there were a lot of hurdles that came in the life of Bill and his family at first instance it was very difficult for Bill to find a permanent job in the city, but slowly and gradually he too succeeded in it. Bill finally find a permanent job as a Mechanical Engineer in a big factory. This was the turning point for Bill's family because after this the family never face any financial crises. The journey and the hardship are shown in more detail in the context of the story.

Darker Truth of Success

The news of getting a sudden promotion in the headquarters made both Daisy and Jennifer dance with joy, They celebrate it as the new journey of their life. The Next day Bill joined the headquarters, since it was a little different job from the factory, at first instance, he found the work difficult, but soon he becomes habituated.

All things were getting smooth.

Daisy started his studies at "Waterfalls Middle School,

Jennifer started a home-based business

and Bill getting promoted year after year.

But as the god is not always great to his children, there was a great turn in the life of Bill's family, as Bill was the only employee from the factory to be part of headquarter, it made Sam and other employees of the company felt jealous about him, as a result, group of employees from the factory-made a master plan against him, they decided to rob the honor of the Bill in front of Senior Officer,

For this, according to the plan Bill was supposed to be called in the factory by Sam who was his best friend for a meet regarding the factory business purpose,

The day arrived and all the thing was according to their plan, after his arrival Sam meet Bill with a very kind gesture showing that he was very happy for his friend's success, Bill couldn't recognize the real face of Sam as he was an innocent man, That day all the other factory employees were on the leave according to the plan.

Sam, Bill, and the merchant were all alone in the factory. Bill as now was an experienced man. He deals with the merchant with much caution and care, but Bill was now all in the trap in the master plan of his colleagues, after much interrogation with the merchant, Bill with no doubt rejected the proposal, as the terms and conditions of the merchant was not matching with the terms and condition of the factory, as merchant received the negative reaction from him, he tried a different way by giving bribe to convince him for the proposal,

He undoubtedly rejected the proposal of receiving any kind of bribes from the merchant. But Sam and the merchant anyhow managed to make Bill touch the money.

This was the movement,

which both merchant and Sam was waiting for,

this movement was captured by Sam and it was sent to the headquarters,

mentioning

"Bill, who used to be an honest man before was now caught by one of his colleagues in the factory for receiving bribes from the merchant".*This kind of uneven activity by Bill made the headquarter department stand amazed, as they know that Bill was not in any condition get to indulge in such activities. But since the department has appropriate prove of Bill's crime, as well as Sam as eye- witnessed, the company has no other option rather suspending Bill from his work. Bill was now again back in search of work, it was now getting difficult for the family to afford "Waterfalls Middle School", Since Jennifer was the only one earning member in the house.*

Jennifer mind was hit with the thought which she never wants **"life in the city is very Hard"**

SUMMARY OF CHAPTER 3

News of getting sudden promotion in the headquarters made both Jennifer and Daisy danced with joy. All was going smoothly with the family but this was not for a long time. There was a great turn in the life of Bill's family, as Bill was the only employee from the factory to be part of headquarter, it made other employees of the company felt jealous about him along with his best friend Sam. A group of employees from the factory made a master plan against him, they decided to rob the honor of the Bill in front of senior officers. As a result, Bill was suspended from his job. The family reached the same condition from where they have started.

Onset Of Extreme Hard Work

Bill and his family were now going through a tough time. But they never lose hope, Even without having a permanent job, Bill was able to make Daisy be a part of "Waterfalls Middle School".Days pass by and all thing goes, as usual, Bill works harder and harder. Soon with many hardships and struggles Bill finally started fresh as an entrepreneur while working hard in multiple jobs. And slowly and gradually he made a good empire from his business. This time there is a sudden rise in the standard of the family, which was much above the normal citizen of Domino City, Bill was now not under any officers, he was the one and the only owner of his company. This time Bill was a bit cautious about the friendzone, as he didn't want to repeat the same mistake which he has committed before. But now all things go well for the Bill family. Bill and his family were now finally living the life which they want.

Since the bill was now a renowned personality of Domino City, there was a lot of enemy of him. But this time Bill was cautious about it. Days pass by, and soon Daisy completed his graduation from one of the renowned universities of Domino City.

As Daisy completed his studies, Bill's mind was hit with the thought which almost all fathers are worried about their children,

"This was regarding the marriage of Daisy"

SUMMARY OF CHAPTER 4

Due to the trap from his colleague Bill and his family were now going through a very tough time. But they never lose hope. With many hardships and struggles, Bill finally started fresh as an entrepreneur while working hard in multiple jobs. And slowly and gradually he made a good empire from his business. All were getting smooth with the family but new trouble was waiting for them now.

Peer For Groom

Daisy completed her final studies and was now thinking to find a good job as she was knowing from her experience how a job is extremely useful for survival, but during this thought, Bill and Jennifer entered Daisy's room and present the thought of marriage before Daisy, by telling her that

"Daisy You might lose us in future, as future is unpredicted, we want you to marry before we finally close our eyes".

Daisy's eyes were filled with tears while listening to such things from her parents, after wiping her face from the tissue which was placed beside the table.

She replied- **"Mom, Dad why you both are saying this, I want both of you in my entire journey of life. So never and ever say like that. I want many things from my life, getting married is not my priority now, I want to be an independent woman, marriage will ruin all my goals."**

Bill- **"Good to see you my daughter that you have grown up now, But all the things which you mentioned can also be accompanied with marriage. But if you want to skip it, then surely we are not going a part of it".**

After much discussion Daisy was now ready for the marriage not because of her own will, but for the pleasure of her parents.

Bill and Jennifer were extremely happy after listening to this. On the following day itself, Bill started to find the best groom for her daughter, In one of the official meetings Bill met accidentally with Alex, who was counted as one of the richest men of Domino City,

Both Bill and Alex have a long conversation that day since both of them were in the same profession,

*During the conversation, Alex accidentally placed a thought of the wedding of his son **"Samson"**.*

Bill was extremely happy to listen that Alex was also looking for a bride for his son. He smartly made Alex realized that he was also looking for a groom for his daughter. Since it was a good proposal from both sides, no one rejected it, and finally, their marriage was supposed to be held in starting of the next month. By fixing the marriage without the proper approval of Daisy, Daisy will surely be going to suffer a lot in the future.

SUMMARY OF CHAPTER 5

Since Bill and Jennifer were worried about Daisy's marriage so they placed the thought of marriage before Daisy. After much discussion Daisy becomes ready for the marriage not because of her own will, but for the pleasure of her parents. But this decision was bringing a big change in her life. Detailed information is mentioned in the context of the story.

Daisy's Marriage

As per schedule wedding was held in the **first week of December on 12th December 2011.** *Since Daisy was the one and only daughter of Bill, Bill made his best to take care of all the guests in the scene. Since Bill's standard was high, the ceremony was attended by big celebs, officers, his employees, and his favorite friend Sam, who directly or indirectly help Bill in acquiring the position where he is now. Sam was very much ashamed of him, as because the crime which he has committed is unforgivable, he even failed to see Bill,*

But Bill forgot all the experience and started fresh with Sam. Sam was extremely happy after seeing this, he apologizes to Bill and all the misconceptions ended between them.

But besides this, there was something uneven happening on the opposite side.

The guest which was invited from the groom's side doesn't reflect the standard of Alex, the arrangement that was supposed to be done by the groom's side was also not up to the mark. Even Samson was not well dressed, this was a shocking experience for Bill and his family. But as there were many guests all around no one questioned against this.

Finally with many ups and down marriage ceremony was completed.

SUMMARY OF CHAPTER 6

Since Daisy was agreed to her marriage, so as per schedule wedding was held in the first week of December on 12th December 2011. The ceremony was attended by big celebs, officers as Bill was a renowned personality in the city. But there was something uneven happening on the opposite side.

Real Face Of Samson

Daisy started her new journey of life with Samson,she was welcomed in the **"Graceview Estate"**. *She was very happy at the beginning, as she in her whole life till now never seen any Estate. But things did not go normal all the time, she noticed that Samson was not respected even by his father and anyone in the house, at first instance she didn't realize why it is so, but slowly and gradually she get to know about it, This was all because Samson was not in any way act as a helping hand for the family rather he was just a sin for them.*

That day she thought that she has made a very big mistake in her life by choosing Samson as her life partner.

But since she has made a final move by choosing him as her life partner, she did her best to convince him to even do any kind of work, because self-respect is very important in life.

But that day she gets to know his real face.

He reacts very violently to her,

and said, **"Who are you to tell me what to do and what not to do in my life and I will live as per my wish. If you are not liking the way I am, leave me and go from where you have come".***By listening to this Daisy got very upset, and thought to discuss this with elders.*

But elders too reacted negatively in this respect, and said- **"We can't do anything in this respect, its is your and Samson problem "** *on the following day itself, she made a call to her father and explain all the scenario which was going in the "Graceview Estate".Bill and Jennifer both were surprised to listen to that . The Next day, Bill and Jennifer came to "Graceview Estate" to know what was going on there.*

But Samson and his family appear before Daisy's parents as nothing has happened, it was all just a miss conception that Daisy has developed in his mind. Bill and Jennifer were amazed to listen that, since her daughter was now a part of someone else house, so they prefer to keep quiet about it and return home the following day itself.

SUMMARY OF CHAPTER 7

After marrying Samson and making him her life partner was a very wrong decision for Daisy which was not only affecting her life but her future generation too. She wonders "it will be better if she persues her career and giving it more important than marriage. Altogether marriage has ruined her life. All detailed information is mentioned in the context of the chapter.

Extreme Phase of Agony

On the way of returning home Bill's mind hit with the thought - **"We had done a big mistake by choosing Samson as Daisy's life partner.**

<u>Jennifer</u>-I agreed with you, but since we cannot change anything now, we are finger-crossed and hoped that all things go well with Daisy.

It is almost two years now and Bill hasn't received any negative reaction of Samson from Daisy.
They thought that all was going normal now with Daisy, but this was not the reality.

It was a starting week from December, Bill as usually was going to read the newspaper on his lawn with a cup of tea in his right hand, and eye-wear in his left,
Jennifer was busy arranging books of Bill's on his bookshelf.
Suddenly, they received a phone call from Daisy, since both of them were very close to her, they left all the work aside and ran to talk to her.
Bill picked up the call, there was a normal conversation between the two for the next few minutes, But after ten minutes suddenly the tone of Bill becomes very low as if he has listened to something different which he has not supposed to listen to.
This kind of gesture attitude of Bill worried Jennifer in the scene.

Jennifer demanded the phone call from Bill so that she could know what was happening there, but Bill rejected the proposal and keep his conversation active for the next one hour.

After an hour Bill keeps the phone aside, with eyes filled with tears, and said "God is really very uncertain to us, I think we are being cursed by our ancestors for not living in the village, That's why they are creating a lot of difficulty in our life.

Jennifer-*Please doesn't make me worried more and come to the direct issue? What is happening there?*

Bill-*On the whole conversation of an hour Daisy keeps on saying to me that she is not going to spend the rest of his life with Samson. In the conversation, she describes to me all the circumstances that had made her take such a step.*

She describes Samson "In my life, I have never come across with such person. He is not a person to become someone's life partner, It's almost four years since our marriage and till now he didn't do anything, whenever I interrogate him about this, he changes the topic every time, he often tortures me with no reason whenever he drinks, Not only this Dad,elders don't listen to a word about there child, even they have told me to ask you to manage all the glossary cost from this month itself, and I am not going to make my future generation to get in this troublesome world.

I am not going to live here anymore, I am coming home soon Dad.

Jennifer-*It's our bad luck that we choose Samson as our daughter's life partner, But the situation goes this only with every woman out there, one has to manage this out.*

Bill- *How you can say that, are you not worried about her?*

Jennifer- *Daisy has to accept this, otherwise late in the future how she could take care of her child as being a single parent.*

Bill- *I think you are right, But?*

Jennifer- *No conversation now, make yourself free tomorrow from your busy schedule, we are going to Graceview Estate tomorrow , whatever we can we will do from our end and leave rest with god.*

SUMMARY OF CHAPTER 8

Bill and Jennifer realized that they have made a big mistake in choosing Samson as Daisy's life partner, but knowing all this they made their mind busy in thinking positive approach to it. But all was vain. Since Samson and his family were not changing in any way. But they tried their best to convince the family.All the detailed information is mentioned in the context of the chapter.

Birth Of Oliver

As per the plan, Bill free himself for a day,
and he along with his wife Jennifer came to the Graceview estate in
the afternoon.

By discussing the issue with Alex and his family they too received a
negative reply in this respect.

<u>Alex</u>-*She has to live according to the way we want, if she doesn't*
want she can leave now itself.

Jennifer and Bill entered Daisy room,

Daisy was sitting in the chair with eyes full of tears which appears as
if she has been crying for many hours, her face gets red and blotchy,
his voice cracked whenever she tries to speak.
these circumstances made Bill forgot all the things which they have
decided before coming to "Graceview Estate" and he finally made up
his plan to take Daisy now itself back to their own house.

<u>Jennifer</u>- *Bill keep patience and let me talk to her.*

<u>Daisy</u>-*Mom, I am not going to live anymore here, please take me*
back home.

_Jennifer__-It is all a part of life, you should give a one more try as because the decision which you want to take is very difficult, might ruin your future, I am not forcing you if the situation still not improves, you surely take the decision which you want but not too early._

Years after years pass by.

**D**aisy gives birth to a child, who was later named "Oliver".who was next after her who was going to suffer in the estate.
Daisy thought that Samson and his family will develop a change in attitude after having a small prince in their family, but the situation was opposite to it.
No one in the family was worried for Oliver except his mother,

In the hospital where Daisy give birth to her child no one from the Graceview estate came to look after her,as the whole family has an assumption that Hospital will make the family ill,

On the other side, Bill and Jennifer was always there to look after Daisy,and their grandson "Oliver"
Bill and Jennifer made their best to take care of them in any condition.
The scene created by Samson and his family was now not new to them, But thinking about the society and the difficulty of living alone forced them to again convince Daisy.

After a week Daisy was back from the hospital. Years pass by, and Bill made his best to take care of his children.

Daisy(thinking)-Why God is so unfortunate to their child!

SUMMARY OF CHAPTER 9

Daisy gives birth to a child, who was later named "Oliver".who was next after her who was going to suffer in the estate. Before it was just Daisy who was suffering in the Estate but after the birth of "Oliver", He was also suffering for the same as no one in the family was worried about him. All detailed information is mentioned in the context of the chapter.

How Difficult is Moving Alone

As Samson was not supporting Daisy in any way, as a result, she made up his mind and finally decided to start a new journey of life being single, because she doesn't want her generation to get all the pain which she has faced in his life. But the journey of moving alone is very difficult in today's world, she faced many hardships at each place as being single, but her current determination always boosted her.

(telephonic conversation between Bill and Daisy)

Daisy-*Dad! I have left Graceview estate a day before and I have started my new journey of life,I could not manage Samson anymore in my life. I am in "The Galaxy" city and looking for a job, and I am pretty sure that I will found out a good job soon.*

Bill-*Daughter!It will be good if you come home and work from here.*

Daisy-*No Dad, I want to be an independent woman, So please Dad now don't ruin my goals.*

Bill-*Sure my daughter! But if you need me at any point in time, please let me know God bless you!*

Daisy was now all alone in "The Galaxy" city, so this time as being an independent woman she was going to bring the best version of herself. Since she was an educated woman she was looking for work that offers a job with higher studies, she came across many MNCs but since she was a single woman all the company rejected her job profile. Day passes by and it was getting tougher for Daisy to bear "The Galaxy City" with savings. But as hardworking is in the gene of the family they never look back, after a week she again applied in an "Automotive" MNC and she was finally selected.

She started to give her best for the company and as a result company sales boosted up, she was promoted year after year and finally a day come when she was chosen as a partner in the company. She was now finally settled,

She made Oliver study in a big school where she was always wanted him to be.

SUMMARY OF CHAPTER 10

Since life was not good with Samson, Daisy made up his mind and finally decided to start the new journey of life. A lot of hurdles came in the life of Daisy in this journey but her current determination always boosted her. All the detailed information is mentioned in detail in the context of the chapter.

Journey Of Transformation

The decision of leaving the Graceview Estate always pleasant Daisy's mind, as because directly or indirectly it helps her to achieve something big in her life independently. She was now a big personality in the city, so she was always in the headlines of the newspaper, which always made Bill and Jennifer proud of her daughter. Oliver was also very proud of her mother and often get appreciated by her friends in his school but his mind was always hit with a single thought that when he is going to meet his father. While reaching home he asks to his mother.

<u>Oliver-</u>*Mom, when I am going to meet my father.*

Daisy (smiled) and said come and have your meal son.

Revealing The Truth

Oliver was very upset as his mother was not responding to him about the question which he has asked her in the evening, she always change the topic whenever he questioned her. But Oliver was his son who was not in any way going to forget it.

At the dinner, he again asked Daisy about his father but this time he asked indirectly to her.

Oliver-Mom, Do you know tomorrow there is an exhibition in our school where all fathers of their respective children are called to the school premises, to present some exciting projects before the judges. One who wins the exhibition, will receive a cash prize along with a gift hamper. I want to be part of it, but I even don't know that when I am going to meet my father?

Daisy- why you are worried my son, you are going to be a part of it, I will come with you, are we are surely winning the Exhibition.

Oliver- No Mom, you can't be a part of it. The children must represent only with their father.

Daisy-Don't worry my child I will talk to your principal and I am sure that she will allow us.

<u>Oliver-</u> *Mom, Please don't hide anything from me now I want to know that why I don't have my father with me, and why he is not living with us.*

<u>Daisy-</u> *Do you want to know what is the matter. Then okay I am going to tell you. It was December month in the year 2011, the day on which I got married to your father "Samson".I never forgot that day as because I have made a very wrong decision in my life. He was not a good person and was not respecting me in any way. That's all, You are so small to know more. So, brush your teeth and go to bed now.*

<u>Oliver</u>- *But Mom I want to know more.*

<u>Daisy-</u> *No conversation now.*

The Exhibition Day

Oliver was ready for the exhibition but was worried about his selection for it. But rather these all thoughts, he made his mind busy thinking that when he will get to know the rest part of her mother life.

On reaching school, Daisy talked with the principal, and finally, she was allowed to represent in place of his husband. But Oliver was worried that his friends will make fun of him as he represent himself with his mother in the exhibition but the situation was opposite to it. All his friends congratulate him for acting different and giving more importance to mothers. Judges were quite impressed with Oliver and his mother, as a result, there were awarded a cash prize of INR 5000 for being the first position in the exhibition.

All his friends came one by one near Oliver and congratulate him for his victory. But Oliver didn't say a word, not because of his pride, rather he was in the different world of knowing the rest part of her mother's life.

Daisy was amazed to see that Oliver didn't spell a word in front of his friends.

While reaching home Oliver threw his medal on the sofa and sat beside it as if someone has scolded him.

Daisy- _What's the matter, Oliver? Why you have thrown your medal. Throwing a medal is the disrespect of success. You should better take it up now._

Oliver- _I am sorry Mom if I disrespect anything, I don't have any intention for it but I am very depressed now, even I am not realizing what I am doing._

_Oliver-__Mom, I have got a pain in my head can you please massage my head._

_Daisy-__Sure my son._

Daisy keeps on asking him that what he is thinking in his mind that create a pain in his head, but Oliver continues his theory of not speaking a word.

Daisy realized that he is thinking of his father and want to know more about him.

Oliver Came To Know The Truth

As over thing was affecting Oliver's health, so Daisy decided to tell all about her life to Oliver.
It was the first time in life for Oliver to listen to a thing with so much concentration.

Daisy started to reside his experience and the life with her husband slowly and calmly with Oliver. Oliver listens patiently to it, till her mother completes. After the completion Daisy find tears in the eyes of Oliver and said-

Why you are crying, my son? That's the reason I was not telling you the whole scenario.

<u>Oliver-</u>No Mom, This is not the tears, the story just made me a little nervous. It was a bad moment for you mother I appreciate what you did. Even if I were in that condition I would have also done the same.

<u>Daisy-</u> Okay Oliver as you know all about me now, please don't hamper your health anymore and get back to sleep.

<u>Oliver-</u> Okay Mom.

Oliver closes his eyes and keeps his mind busy in thinking --

"Why does god always keep on checking his children, I will always be with my mother and whatever I can I will do with my end."

Uncertain Decision

The Next Morning, While having a cup of tea on her veranda Daisy's mind hit with a thought which change their life This was regarding Samson.

<u>Daisy-(thinking)</u> *Oliver as a child misses his father more and finds himself incomplete as compared to his friends,* **<u>what if I give a try to "Samson" for Oliver's happiness.</u>**

During this thought suddenly Oliver entered the scene.

<u>Oliver-</u>*Good morning Mummy.*

<u>Daisy-</u>*Good morning my son, as it is Sunday morning, the day on which we both are free, So brush up your teeth fast and be ready we are going somewhere.*

<u>Oliver-</u>*Where Mummy.*

<u>Daisy-</u>*It's a surprise, my son.*

Oliver Reached Graceview Estate

As it was a surprise trip from his mother's end, Oliver made himself ready as fast as he can, after having some sandwiches along with mango juice they started their journey at around 10 'O' clock. After a big journey of almost 4 hours, they reaches their destination and came to a different city which was familiar to Daisy, but it was a new place for Oliver as it was **"Domino City".**

As Oliver didn't know the exact city of his birthplace so he considered "Domino City" as a normal place for their holiday trip. After reaching Domino City the Driver's drive throws rocky mountains, greenery, and reach a place which was so beautiful that no one could ignore its beauty, this was **"Graceview Estate".***Before entering the Estates she tells Oliver all about it. After knowing more about Graceview Estate Oliver drop the plan of entering it and insist his mother return, but Daisy wanted him to know about the truth practically. After much negotiation between the two Oliver finally agreed to enter the estate.*

Oliver Met His Father

After entering the Graceview Estate all were amazed to see Daisy and his success journey.Since Daisy was a big personality in the scenario, as a result now she was respected much than before, but this time she didn't come to live in an Estate rather she came there just for a sake of convenience for Oliver to know the reality.

Oliver-*Mom where we are now.*

Daisy-*We are in Graceview Estate and we have come here to meet your father.*

Oliver-*It is very bad mom, why we are here I didn't want to meet my father anymore.*

Daisy- *It is very bad to judge someone so early my son we will just meet him and leave Graceview Estate as soon as possible.*

Oliver-*Ok Mom.*

To Be continued........................

Glossary

Chirping	short sharp sound
Obessive	Thinking too much.
Eulogize	To praise somebody
hustle & bustle	busy world
Ample	Enough
Glimpse	A very quick view
Global Corporation Company	Fictional Company
Domino City	Fictional City
Bribe	illegally money
indulge	involved
Graceview Estate	Fictional Estate
troublesome	causes trouble
Unfortunate	not lucky
veranda	a platform of a house
Automotive MNC	Fictional MNC

www.ingramcontent.com/pod-product-compliance
Lightning Source LLC
LaVergne TN
LVHW050426160726
843469LV00041B/1245